TEDDY Spaghetti

Written by **Dorothea Benton Frank** and **Victoria Benton Frank**

Illustrated by **Renée Andriani**

HARPER

An Imprint of HarperCollinsPublishers

Teddy Spaghetti

Text copyright © 2020 by Dorothea Benton Frank and Victoria Frank Peluso

Illustrations copyright © 2020 by Renée Andriani

All rights reserved. Manufactured in China.

No part of this book may be used or reproduced in any manner whatsoever without written permission

except in the case of brief quotations embodied in critical articles and reviews. For information address

HarperCollins Children's Books, a division of HarperCollins Publishers, 195 Broadway, New York, NY 10007.

www.harpercollinschildrens.com

Library of Congress Control Number: 2019944198

ISBN 978-0-06-291542-9

The artist used Photoshop to create the digital illustrations for this book.

Typography by Rachel Zegar. Hand lettering by Renée Andriani.

20 21 22 23 24 SCP 10 9 8 7 6 5 4 3 2 1

❖

First Edition

For Peter and Carmine and the real
Teddy Spaghetti, with all our love
—D.F. and V.F.

For my pasta aficionados, Maggie, Ellen, and Joe.
May your noodles always be al dente.
—R.A.

Teddy loved a lot about his life, but he really loved three simple things.

He loved his shiny cape (because it made him feel big and strong).

He really loved his rain boots (because when he wore them, Teddy could stomp through anything).

But most of all, Teddy really, really, really loved spaghetti (because . . . well . . . just because).

He loved spaghetti so much he wanted to eat it for breakfast, lunch, and dinner.

He would slurp it,

twirl it,

and gobble it up.

He liked spaghetti with red
sauce and meatballs . . .

with white sauce and clams . . .

or even with eggs and bacon!

Teddy was a very happy boy, and today was a very important day. He was starting a new school. And as much as his shiny cape made him feel confident, he felt a teensy, tiny bit nervous.

"Good morning, Teddy. It's a big day," said his mom. "Are you ready for a big breakfast?"

"Can I have spaghetti?" asked Teddy.

"Not today, my sweet boy," replied his mom.

"I think I'm feeling a little under the weather," said Teddy.

"You're going to be just fine, kiddo. I bet you'll have a new best friend by lunchtime."

Teddy was not so sure.

"Mom, I don't feel so good!
"My elbow hurts, my leg hurts, I have a pain in my neck! My eyes are blurry! My tummy's sick. Maybe I have a fever? I might have appendicitis. I'm hot. I'm cold! My blood pressure's through the roof!"

"Teddy, you'll be just fine! Just be your wonderful self and everyone will love you. Now, hand over your cape and let's get moving," said Mom.

Teddy didn't feel great about handing over his trusted cape, but he did it anyway. He grabbed his lunch box and headed out the door.

He said goodbye to his mom and walked slowly up to the front of the school.

"Welcome, Teddy!" said his new teacher, Ms. Basil. "Are you ready to meet everyone?"

"Ready as I'll ever be," said Teddy with a smile.

Teddy said slowly, "I ate a lot of spaghetti!"

"You must really like spaghetti! What's your name?" asked the girl sitting next to him.

"I'm Theodore, but everyone calls me Teddy, and I don't just really like spaghetti, I love it!" he said.

"Well, I'm Antonia, but everyone calls me Toni. And this is Petey."

Teddy was relieved that he had met some friends he could sit with at lunch. The new friends found a table together.

Petey looked at his lunch and said, "A jelly sandwich. This meal is uninspired."

Toni said, "Bologna, bologna, always with the bologna. Ugh."

Teddy opened his container and smiled. The smell of spaghetti made him think of home . . . in a good way.

Just then, he heard a loud, booming voice.

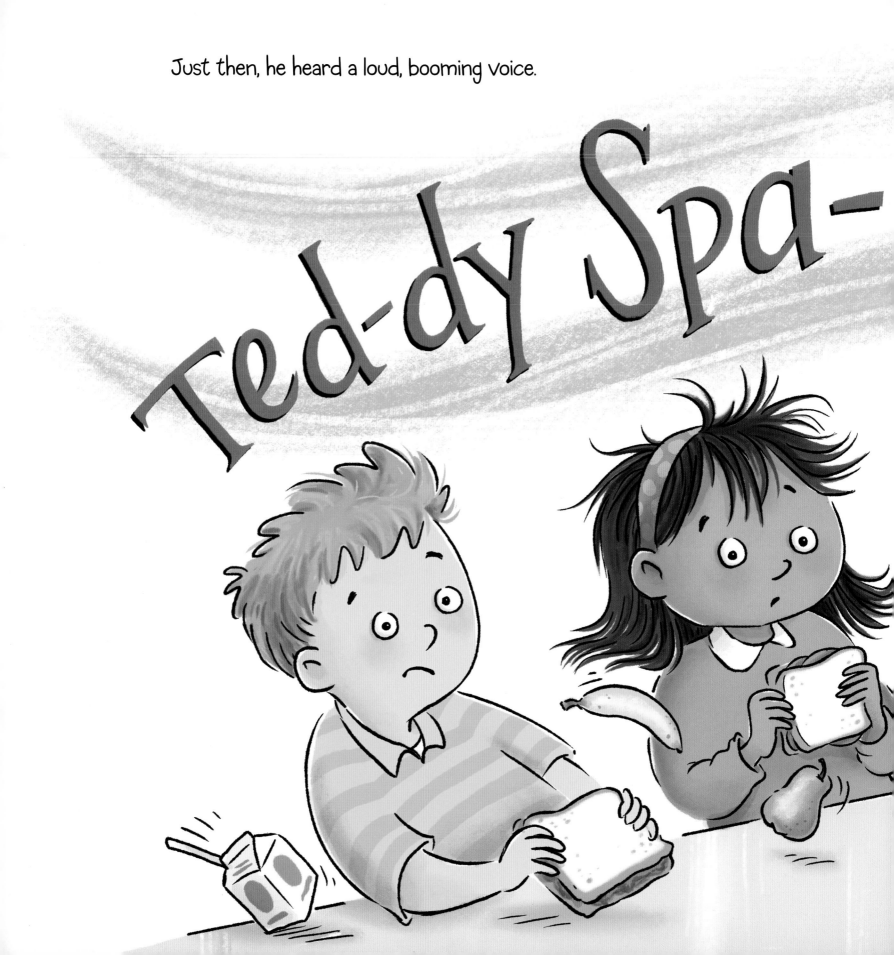

It was Bryan the Bully.

Teddy forgot for a moment that he was the new kid and that Bryan was much bigger than him.

"Hey, what did you call me?" asked Teddy.

Bryan the Bully spoke more slowly this time . . .
"I called you

TEDDY SPA-GHETTI!"

Teddy felt his heart sink. He wasn't sure what to say next.

But he didn't need to say anything because his new friends spoke up.

Teddy told everyone to help themselves.
"There's plenty to go around."

Suddenly, it was quiet again. Teddy turned around to find Bryan standing over him, but this time he didn't look quite so mean.

"Can I have some spaghetti?" he asked, almost in a whisper.

Teddy thought for a moment. He looked up at Bryan and smiled.

"Sure! And you can call me Teddy Spaghetti, because I like that name a lot! No, wait. I love that name! Almost as much as I love spaghetti!"

Everyone gathered around and enjoyed the spaghetti, down to the last slurp.

Even Bryan!

That night his mom said, "Teddy, I'm so glad you had a good day. What do you want for lunch tomorrow?"

Teddy knew the answer right away.
"Spaghetti . . . with extra forks!"